BUSY BUSY!

by LUCY SCOTT

Creston Books

I'm not sleepy. I'm just having a little rest.

I had a Busy Busy day!

I learned how socks work!
I can put them on and take
them off all by myself.

Daddy's sock made a nice hat
but it was a bit smelly.

I had a BUSY BUSY day!

I had breakfast at the zoo!

We ate pear, porridge, and pancakes with blueberries.
I had to feed bunny because she's only little.

I had a Busy Busy day!

I built a city!

Teddy and Zebra Rabbit wanted a high-up house with a good view, Doggy was a little bit scared and decided to live on the floor.

I had a Busy Busy day!

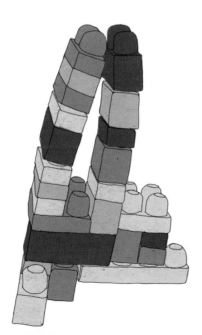

I made lots and lots of pictures!

I drew Mommy, then I painted Daddy, then Rosie the Pussycat, then flowers (with lots of bees), a silly billy, a potty, and a horse (which was tricky).

Mommy said she loved the paintings that were on paper but didn't like the ones on the floor so much.

I had a Busy Busy day!

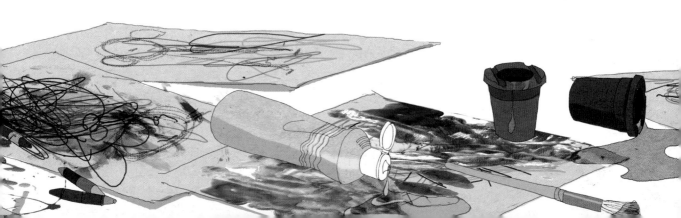

I cooked lunch for ten!

Pat the Dog is a VERY picky eater, Piggy is so greedy, and Zebra Rabbit would only eat lettuce. Everyone wanted something different.

I barely had time to eat my own lunch!

I had a Busy Busy day!

I hunted for treasure! I found all sorts of wonderful things. I found red jewels, green jewels, shiny things, and sparkly stuff.

I searched and I searched but I couldn't find piggy.

I had a Busy Busy day!

I crossed a river full of crocodiles!

I didn't just cross once – I had to get
all my friends across safely too!
I was very brave.

I had a Busy Busy day!

I made up a new tune!

I call it the shaky BANG tinkle, clickety-click wooooooop wooooOOOOOOOoooop song.

Rosie the Pussycat loves it when I make music.

I had a Busy Busy day!

I had a jungle adventure!

I met a scary leopard who was having a little rest after a big run and a cuddly panda who liked telling jokes.

"What's black and white and likes to eat bamboo? A silly penguin!"

I had a Busy Busy day!

All my friends came to dinner,
I taught them how to eat spaghetti.
They were very impressed!

I had a Busy Busy day!

I washed the faces of 3 dolphins,
2 ducks, 1 whale, 1 hippo,
1 crab, 1 baby, and
1 very dirty penguin.

Good thing my own face wasn't dirty!

I had a Busy Busy day!

And after all that, I rode a camel across a sandy desert.

I had a Busy Buszzzzzz. . .

Lucy Scott has drawn every day for as long as she can remember. She studied drawing and painting at the Edinburgh College of Art. In 2005 Lucy and her partner Tom founded Treehouse24, a storyboard and animatic company.

After giving birth to her first child, Lucy used the experience as the basis for *Doodle Diary of a New Mom*. Excerpts from the book appeared in many online magazines and newspapers including *The Huffington Post*. Within a week, the images had gone viral, notching up 2.5 million views on *Buzzfeed* alone.

Busy Busy, her first book for children, was inspired by her 2 year-old daughter's boundless imaginative play and relentless energy.

Lucy lives in Edinburgh with her partner Tom and daughter Lois. She is currently working on her second children's book, she continues to storyboard, and, best of all, loves being a mother. You can learn more about Lucy at lucyscottpictures.com, facebook.com/doodlediaryofanewmum, and twitter.com/lucyspictures.